Anne of Green Gables

L.M. Montgomery

Condensed and Adapted by
MARGARET DeKEYSER

Illustrated by
JERRY DILLINGHAM

Cover Illustrated by
LEE WING PAINTING WORKSHOP

bendon

The Junior Classics have been
adapted and illustrated with care and thought
to introduce you to a world of famous authors, characters, ideas,
and great stories that have been loved for generations.

Editor — Kathryn Knight
Creative Director — Gina Rhodes Haynes
And the entire classics project team

ANNE OF GREEN GABLES

Copyright © 2014 Bendon
Ashland, Ohio 44805 • 1-888-5-BENDON
bendonpub.com

Printed in the United States of America

A note to the reader—

A classic story rests in your hands. The characters are famous. The tale is timeless.

This Junior Classic edition of *Anne of Green Gables* has been carefully condensed and adapted from the original version (which you really *must* read when you're ready for every detail). We kept the well-known phrases for you. We kept L. M. Montgomery's style. And we kept the important imagery and heart of the tale.

Literature is terrific fun! It encourages you to think. It helps you dream. It is full of heroes and villains, suspense and humor, adventure and wonder, and new ideas. It introduces you to writers who reach out across time to say: "Do you want to hear a story I wrote?"

Curl up and enjoy.

CONTENTS

CHARACTERS

ANNE SHIRLEY — the young orphan who comes to live with the Cuthberts

MATTHEW AND **MARILLA CUTHBERT** — the middle-aged brother and sister who own the Green Gables farm in Avonlea, Prince Edward Island, Canada

MRS. RACHEL LYNDE — a neighbor of the Cuthberts, one of Avonlea's most upstanding (and nosiest) citizens

MRS. ALEXANDER SPENCER — helps the Cuthberts when they decide to adopt an orphan

MRS. THOMAS — took Anne in after her parents died

THE HAMMONDS — the second family (with eight children!) that Anne lived with

MRS. PETER BLEWETT — offers to take Anne in if the Cuthberts don't want to keep her

CHARACTERS

DIANA BARRY — Anne's best friend

MRS. BARRY — Diana's mother

MINNIE MAY — Diana Barry's younger sister

MR. PHILLIPS — Anne's first teacher at the Avonlea school

GILBERT BLYTHE — one of the best students at school and Anne's chief rival

MR. AND MRS. ALLAN — the new minister at Avonlea and his wife

MISS MURIEL STACY — Avonlea's first lady school teacher

JOSIE PYE — a classmate of Anne's who likes to give her a hard time

RUBY GILLIS AND JANE ANDREWS — two of Anne's friends at school

Anne of
Green Gables

CHAPTER ONE

A Surprise at Green Gables

Mrs. Rachel Lynde was a nosy neighbor, but good-hearted. She kept an eye on everything that happened in Avonlea. One afternoon in early June, she sat looking out her window. She saw Matthew Cuthbert heading out of town in his buggy, dressed in his best clothes. Now, where was he going dressed up like that and why?

After tea, Mrs. Lynde went over to Green Gables to see Marilla Cuthbert, Matthew's sister. They had lived on neighboring farms for many years. The two women couldn't be more different. Mrs. Rachel Lynde was plump and outspoken and nosy. Marilla was thin and quiet and kept mostly to herself.

Mrs. Lynde asked where Matthew had gone. Marilla told her that he went to pick up the orphan boy they were adopting. She explained that when they heard that Mrs. Alexander Spencer was going to adopt a little girl from the orphanage, she and Matthew sent a message to her. They asked her to pick out a boy about eleven years old for them. Matthew was getting older and they thought a boy could help him with the farm chores. Today Matthew had gone to the train station to bring the boy home to their farm, Green Gables.

Mrs. Rachel Lynde was shocked. She could not picture serious Marilla and shy Matthew as the parents of a child. She did not approve of adopting orphans, either. It was "foolish," she said, and "risky." She told Marilla awful stories about orphans who caused lots of trouble. There was a boy who set the house on fire and another, a girl, who poisoned the whole family.

"Well, we're not getting a girl," said Marilla firmly. "And besides, Matthew has his mind set on this. And as for the risk, there are risks with having one's own children."

Meanwhile, Matthew had arrived at the train station. There was no sign of a train. Matthew spoke to the stationmaster and told him he was picking up an orphan boy. The man pointed to the far end of the train platform. A thin child sat there on a stack of roofing shingles, clutching a shabby little carpetbag.

"There was a passenger dropped off for you, but it is a little girl," the stationmaster said.

"I'm not expecting a girl," said Matthew. "It's a boy I've come for."

The stationmaster whistled. "Guess there's been some mistake. Go ask her."

Matthew walked down the train platform toward the girl. She was a child of about eleven, dressed in a very short and ugly yellow dress and a faded brown sailor hat. Her red hair hung down her back in thick braids. She was very thin, with large green eyes sparkling in her freckled face. She stood up and stuck out her hand to Matthew.

"Are you Mr. Matthew Cuthbert of Green Gables?" she asked. "I was afraid you weren't coming for me. I was imagining all the things that could have happened to keep you away. Then I saw that big cherry tree down the tracks.

I thought if you didn't come, I would walk down there. I could climb up in the tree and spend the night in the branches. Wouldn't it be nice to sleep in a cherry tree all covered with blossoms? And I knew that you would come in the morning if you didn't come tonight."

Matthew shook her hand. He decided to take her home even though she was a girl. He couldn't tell her there had been a mistake. Matthew decided that they could sort it out later, at home. "I'm sorry I was late," he said shyly. "Come along. I'll carry your bag for you."

"Oh, I can carry it," she told him happily. "It has everything I own in it, but it's not heavy at all. It's a long drive to your place, isn't it? Oh, it seems so wonderful that I'm going to live with you! I've never belonged to anybody before."

During the long ride to Green Gables, she did nothing but talk. Matthew liked her company, which was rare for him. He was usually very shy, especially with women and little girls. She talked about her life at the orphanage, and about the red roads and what made them that way, and about pretty dresses with puffed sleeves, and about the trip from the orphanage to

Prince Edward Island on the boat. She even talked about talking too much!

"Would you rather I didn't talk?" she asked Matthew.

"Oh, you can talk as much as you like," Matthew told her.

"I'm so glad. I know you and I are going to be great friends. It's so nice to be able to talk when you want to. People always tell me that children should be seen and not heard, but I don't believe that's true."

She held up one of her thick braids. "What color would you call this?" she asked.

"It's red, ain't it?" Matthew answered.

"Yes, it's red," she sighed. "I don't mind being skinny and having freckles, but I hate my red hair. You just can't be perfectly happy when you have red hair. I wish it was black, but it's just plain old red."

When they got close to Green Gables, they passed by Barry's Pond. The little girl loved the way the water sparkled in the sunset. She thought "Barry's Pond" was too plain a name for such a pretty place. She renamed the pond the Lake of Shining Waters.

"I just love romantic names," she told Matthew. "When I don't like the name of something, I just give it a new name of my own."

After they passed by the Lake of Shining Waters, Matthew said, "We're pretty near Green Gables now."

There ahead, in a little valley, Anne's eye fell on a pretty white house with a green gabled roof.

"Oh, I've been afraid it was all a dream! I thought I'd never have a real home," the child chirped. "But here it is! It's real and we're home!"

Matthew had only spent a little while with this girl and already she had charmed him completely. He dreaded telling the child that she'd have to go back to the orphanage the very next day. Matthew couldn't break her heart that way. He'd leave that to Marilla. Marilla was always better with problems of this sort.

"Matthew Cuthbert, who's that?" Marilla demanded, as they walked into the kitchen. "Where is the boy?"

"There wasn't any boy," said Matthew. "There was only her. The stationmaster said she was dropped off for us. She was all alone. I couldn't just leave her at the station."

12

The child burst into tears. "You don't want me because I'm not a boy!" she cried. "Nobody ever did want me."

Marilla and Matthew didn't know what to say. Neither of them was used to being around children. Finally Marilla said, "There's no need to cry about it."

"Yes, there *is* need!" The child looked up at them through her tears. "You would cry too if you were an orphan and had come to a place you thought was going to be home and then you found out they didn't want you because you're not a boy. This is the *worst* thing that's ever happened to me!"

"Well," said Marilla, "you'll stay here tonight, and tomorrow we'll go to Mrs. Spencer's house and sort this out. What's your name?"

"Anne Shirley," the child answered, "but please call me Cordelia. Anne is such an unromantic name."

"Unromantic fiddlesticks!" said Marilla. "Anne is a good, sensible name."

"Well, if you must call me Anne, please call me Anne spelled with an E. It looks so much nicer that way," the girl requested.

"Very well, Anne spelled with an E, can you tell us how this happened?" Marilla asked, with a hint of a smile. "We sent for a boy. Weren't there any boys at the orphanage?"

"There were plenty of boys, but Mrs. Spencer said you wanted a girl," Anne explained. "She adopted Lily Jones for herself. Lily has beautiful curly brown hair. If I had brown hair, would you keep me?"

"No," Marilla said. "Mrs. Spencer must have been mistaken. We sent her a message, but we should have gone ourselves. We want a boy to help Matthew on the farm. A girl would be of no use to us. Well, we may as well eat, anyway."

Anne was so upset that she couldn't eat much dinner. She just sat and moped all through the meal.

"I guess she's just tired," said Matthew. "Best put her to bed, Marilla."

Marilla lit a candle and told Anne to follow her. They went through the oh-so-clean house to the east gable room. The bedroom was bare and stark white. There were no little girl frills anywhere in it. Anne put on her threadbare nightgown and crawled under the covers of the bed.

"Good night," Marilla said.

"How can you call it a good night?" Anne demanded. "It's the worst night I ever had." She angrily pulled the covers up over her head.

Marilla went back to the kitchen to wash the dishes. "Well, this is a pretty kettle of fish we've landed in," she said. "This girl will have to be sent back to the orphanage."

"Well now, she's a nice little thing, Marilla," said Matthew. "It's kind of a pity to send her back when she's so set on staying here."

"Matthew Cuthbert, you don't mean to say we ought to keep her!" Marilla was surprised.

"We might be some good to her," said Matthew.

"Matthew Cuthbert, I believe that child has enchanted you! I can see as plain as plain that you want to keep her."

"Well now, she's a real interesting little thing," persisted Matthew. "You should have heard her talk coming from the station."

"Oh, she can talk fast enough. I saw that at once. I don't like children who have so much to say. I don't want an orphan girl. And besides, there's something I don't understand about her. No, she's got to be sent back."

"I could hire a boy to help me," said Matthew, "and she'd be company for you."

"I don't need any company," said Marilla. "And I'm not going to keep her."

"Well now, whatever you say, Marilla," said Matthew. "I'm going to bed."

To bed went Matthew. And to bed, when she had put her dishes away, went Marilla, frowning. And upstairs, in the east gable room, a lonely, heartbroken, friendless child cried herself to sleep.

CHAPTER TWO

A New Beginning for Anne

Anne awoke to cheery sunlight streaming through the window. For a moment she could not remember where she was. She felt thrilled—and then she remembered. This was Green Gables and they didn't want her because she wasn't a boy! But it was morning and there was a cherry tree in full bloom outside of her window. It was hard to be sad when everything outside was so beautiful. Tall trees lined the yard. The orchards sloped down to the Lake of Shining Waters and up a hill to the next farm. She could see just the gable end of the neighbor's farmhouse. Everything was buzzing and blooming in the June sunshine.

Marilla came in. "It's time you were dressed," she said.

Anne drew a long breath. "Oh, isn't it wonderful? Everything at Green Gables is so beautiful," she said, waving her hand at the scene outside her window. "Even though I'm so sad that I have to leave today, I'll always remember it. I've just been imagining that you wanted me. I was going to stay here forever and ever. Now I have to stop imagining, and that hurts."

"You'd better get dressed and never mind your imaginings," said Marilla. "Make your bed, then come down to breakfast."

"I'm pretty hungry this morning," Anne announced as she sat down at the table. "The world doesn't seem as bad as it did last night. I'm so glad it's a sunshiny morning. I like rainy mornings real well, too. All sorts of mornings are interesting, don't you think? But it's easier to handle your problems on a sunny day, isn't it?"

"For pity's sake, hold your tongue," said Marilla. "You talk way too much for a little girl. This afternoon, we'll go to Mrs. Spencer's and get this sorted out. There must be some answer to how this mistake was made."

21

After lunch, Matthew hitched up the buggy, and Marilla and Anne set off. Anne talked the whole time they were driving to Mrs. Spencer's. She talked about wild roses and pink dresses and red hair.

"Did you ever know of anybody whose hair was red when she was young, but got to be another color when she grew up?" she asked Marilla.

"No, I don't know as I ever did."

ANNE OF GREEN GABLES

Anne sighed. "Well, another hope gone. Are we going across the Lake of Shining Waters today?"

"We're not going over Barry's Pond, if that's what you mean by your Lake of Shining Waters. We're going by the shore road. Since you're bent on talking, tell me about yourself."

"I was eleven last March," said Anne. "My parents were both teachers. They died of fever when I was just three months old. They had no relatives to take me in, so a neighbor, Mrs. Thomas, said she'd take me. I lived with her family until I was eight years old. I helped look after the children. Then Mr. Thomas was killed and Mrs. Thomas and the children went to live with her mother. There was no room for me. Another lady, Mrs. Hammond, said she'd take me, because I was handy with children. Mrs. Hammond had eight children—can you believe she had three sets of twins? I lived with Mrs. Hammond about two years until Mr. Hammond died in an accident. Mrs. Hammond gave all of her children away to relatives then and moved to the United States. I had to go to the orphanage because nobody would take me. I was there four months until Mrs. Spencer came."

Anne sighed. She did not like talking about a world that had not wanted her.

"Those women," Marilla asked her, "were they good to you?"

"Oh, they meant to be," Anne answered. "They had so much to worry about, you know. But I'm sure they meant to be good to me."

Marilla felt sorry for the child. What a starved, unloved life she had had. She had worked hard for those families, but it was clear they had not given her the love she needed. No wonder she had been so happy at the idea of a real home. It was a pity she had to be sent back.

What if she let her stay? Matthew was set on it and the child was a nice little girl.

They rambled along the shore road with the sandstone cliffs, the scrub firs and the coves strewn with pebbles. Anne rambled on, too.

"Isn't the sea wonderful? Once, Mr. Thomas took us all to the shore. I enjoyed every minute, even though I had to look after the children. I lived it over in happy dreams for years. This shore is nicer. And aren't the seagulls splendid? Would you like to be a seagull? I would."

She talked all the way to Mrs. Spencer's house.

Mrs. Spencer was surprised to see Marilla pull up in the buggy with Anne. She invited them in. Marilla explained that there had been a mistake. They had wanted a *boy*. Mrs. Spencer apologized. She said that the message *she* had received was that they wanted a *girl*. It must have gotten mixed up along the way.

"Can we send her back to the orphanage and get a boy?" Marilla asked.

"Maybe we won't have to send her back," Mrs. Spencer answered. She explained that she had a neighbor, Mrs. Peter Blewett, who wanted to adopt a girl. Mrs. Blewett was tired out from taking care of her large family. She wanted an orphan girl who would work very hard without complaining. Marilla had heard of Mrs. Blewett. People said she was mean and sharp-tongued. The orphan girl she took would have to take care of the children and all the cleaning and cooking and farm chores, too. Marilla didn't like the idea of sending Anne there.

Anne sat listening to them talk. Her eyes burned with tears.

Marilla saw how unhappy Anne looked. She could not send her to that horrible Mrs. Blewett.

"Well," Marilla told Mrs. Spencer, "Matthew wants to keep her. I think I'd better take her home and talk it over with him. If we decide not to keep her, we'll bring her back here tomorrow."

Marilla said nothing to Matthew until they were out behind the barn later that evening. Then she told him Anne's history and about their visit with Mrs. Spencer.

"Matthew," admitted Marilla, "I'm willing to keep her. I've never brought up a child, and I'll probably make a mess of it. But I'll do my best. And Matthew, you're not to meddle. Perhaps an old maid doesn't know much about bringing up a child, but neither does an old bachelor. So you just leave me to manage her."

"There, there, Marilla, you can have your own way," said Matthew. "Only be as kind to her as you can without spoiling her. She'll be a good girl."

The next morning, Marilla kept Anne busy with chores around the house. She could tell that Anne was smart, obedient, and quick to learn. Her only fault seemed to be a tendency to daydream and to forget about the job she was doing at the time.

29

All day long, Anne waited for Marilla to tell her what she had decided. Would Anne stay at Green Gables or go live with the Blewett family? Finally that afternoon, Anne couldn't wait any longer.

"Please, Miss Cuthbert, are you going to keep me or send me back? I've tried to be patient, but I just can't wait any longer to find out," Anne asked anxiously.

"Well," said Marilla, "Matthew and I have decided to keep you. You can stay here and we will try to do right by you."

"Oh, it's like a dream come true!" exclaimed Anne. Happy tears filled her eyes. "I am so glad I can stay here at Green Gables. What should I call you? Do I say Miss Cuthbert all the time or may I call you Aunt Marilla? I've never had an aunt or any relation at all, not even a grandmother."

"No, you'll call me Marilla just like everyone else does."

Later, Anne asked Marilla, "Do you think that I'll ever have a dear friend?"

"Diana Barry lives over at Orchard Slope and she's about your age. She's a very nice little girl. Perhaps she will be a playmate for you."

"What is Diana like? Her hair isn't red, is it? It's hard enough for me to bear my own red hair. I wouldn't want my best friend to have the same problem."

"Diana is a very pretty little girl. She has black hair and rosy cheeks. And she is good and smart, which is better than being pretty." Marilla always liked to include a lesson with anything she said to children.

When Anne went to bed that night in the east gable, she imagined all sorts of things. She pretended that she was a great lady, dressed in silks and pearls. But when she looked in the little mirror, she still saw her own thin, freckled face. She whispered to herself, "You're only Anne of Green Gables. But it's a million times nicer to be Anne of Green Gables than Anne of nowhere special, isn't it?"

CHAPTER THREE

Anne's Apology

When Anne was not doing chores, she explored Green Gables. She made friends with every tree and shrub. She visited the Lake of Shining Waters and danced over the hills and gathered starflowers. She played in the orchard and picked violets in the valley. Anne decorated her little east gable room with apple blossoms and lilacs. She told Matthew and Marilla every last detail of all her wanderings. They grew used to her talkative ways and soon it felt like she'd always been part of life at Green Gables.

Now, Mrs. Rachel Lynde, the nosy neighbor, had been sick. If she'd been well, she would have come right away to meet the orphan. Anne had been at Green Gables for almost two weeks before Mrs. Lynde was well enough to visit. When she finally came, Marilla called Anne in from playing. Her freckles were bright from the sunshine and her red hair was very windblown.

Mrs. Rachel Lynde was a woman who said what she thought. She took one look at Anne and said, "Well, you didn't pick her for her looks, that's for sure. She's a skinny little thing, isn't she? Look at those freckles! And hair as red as carrots, too. Come here, child."

Anne got terribly angry and her face turned bright red. She stomped across the room and yelled at Mrs. Lynde.

"I hate you," she cried. "How dare you call me skinny and ugly? How dare you say I'm freckled and redheaded? You are a rude woman! How would you like to be called fat and clumsy? I don't care if I hurt your feelings! You have hurt mine and I'll *never* forgive you for it! Never! Never! Never!"

Anne stomped her foot in anger.

Mrs. Rachel Lynde was shocked. She didn't say a word. She just sat and stared at Anne.

"Anne, go to your room at once," said Marilla. Marilla's white face looked very angry.

Anne ran up to the east gable. She threw herself onto her bed and cried.

Marilla did not know what to say to Mrs. Lynde. When she spoke, she surprised herself by sticking up for the child. "You shouldn't have teased her about her looks, Rachel. I'm not trying to excuse her. I'll give her a stern talking to about it. But she's never been taught what is right. You were too hard on her, Rachel."

"Well," Mrs. Lynde said, "if I were you, I'd do that 'talking to' with a birch stick!" She swept out the door, very offended.

Marilla found Anne on her bed, crying.

"Anne, get off that bed this minute and listen to me. How could you lose your temper like that? I was ashamed of you, Anne. Rachel was a stranger and a grownup and a guest. You should have been respectful to her for all those reasons. You were very rude. You must go apologize to her."

"I can't," said Anne. "I cannot ask Mrs. Lynde to forgive me."

"She only said things about you that you say about yourself," Marilla said. "You've said that

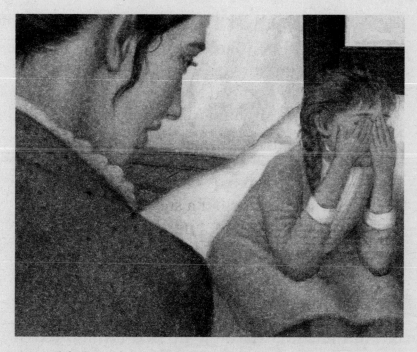

you think you're skinny, and you hate your red hair and freckles."

"It's different," Anne answered, "when someone else says it. It's not the same at all."

"Just the same, you must say you're sorry," said Marilla, "and you'll stay here in your room until you do."

"I'll have to stay here forever then," said Anne. "I'm sorry I upset you, but I can't say I'm sorry when I'm not."

"Well, maybe you'll see it differently in the morning," replied Marilla, "because you'll have all night to think it over."

In spite of herself, Marilla was a little bit amused as she walked down to the kitchen. Mrs. Rachel had been rude and she was an old gossip. It was high time someone pointed those facts out to her.

Anne stayed in her room the whole next day. Marilla brought up her meals, but wouldn't let Anne come down until she was ready to say she was sorry.

Matthew thought it was too quiet downstairs without Anne. After dinner, when Marilla was out in the barn, Matthew tiptoed up to the east gable room. He peeped in, walked over to the unhappy girl, and whispered, "Anne, don't you think you'd better do it and have it over with? You know, Marilla is a mighty determined woman, Anne. Do it, and have it over with."

"Do you mean apologize to Mrs. Lynde?"

"Yes—apologize—that's the very word," said Matthew. "It's terrible lonesome downstairs without you—just go and smooth it over—but don't tell Marilla I've said anything about it."

"Very well," said Anne. "I would never want to make either of you unhappy."

When Marilla came in, she heard Anne calling her from the upstairs hall.

"I'm sorry I said rude things," Anne told her. "I'm ready to go and tell Mrs. Lynde, too."

Marilla took Anne to Mrs. Lynde's house. By the time they got there, Anne had worked up a very special apology. She walked in and got down on her knees at Mrs. Rachel Lynde's feet.

"Oh, Mrs. Lynde, I am so very sorry! It was very wicked of me to fly into a temper because you told me the truth. You were right—my hair *is* red and I'm freckled and skinny. What I said to you was true, too, but I shouldn't have said it. Please, please forgive me. If you won't, it will break the heart of a poor little orphan. You wouldn't want to do that, would you?"

Mrs. Lynde was impressed by this emotional speech. She forgave Anne and they promised to be friends from then on.

On the way home, Anne told Marilla that she wouldn't get so angry if people didn't tease her about her red hair. She was so tired of being teased.

But it does give you a lovely feeling to say you're sorry and be forgiven, doesn't it?" asked Anne. She slipped her hand into Marilla's and told her how happy she was to live at Green Gables. It was the first real home she'd ever had.

CHAPTER FOUR

A New Friend

"Well, how do you like them?" said Marilla.

Anne was standing in the gable room, looking at three new dresses spread out on the bed. Marilla had made them for her. One was brown gingham, one had black and white checks, and one was an ugly blue print. They were all made alike, with plain skirts and plain, tight sleeves. Anne didn't say anything.

"Oh, I can tell you don't like the dresses!" Marilla said impatiently. "What is the matter with them? Why don't you like them? Aren't they neat and clean and new?"

"They're—they're not—pretty," said Anne.

"Pretty!" Marilla said. "I didn't trouble myself about pretty, Anne. Pretty isn't important. Those dresses are good and sensible. They're all you'll get this summer. The brown one and the blue one are for school. The black and white one is for church and Sunday school. Be sure you keep them neat and clean."

"I just wish one of them had puffed sleeves," said Anne. "Puffed sleeves are the fashion, you know. But thank you for making them."

"Well, you'll have to do without puffed sleeves. Puffed sleeves are just a waste of perfectly good fabric. Just vanity! Hang the dresses up in your closet. You're going to Sunday school tomorrow." Marilla went downstairs.

The next morning Marilla had a sick headache and couldn't go to Sunday school with Anne. Anne went off by herself, wearing the black and white checkered dress. Her hat was just as plain as the dress. Anne would have liked ribbons and flowers on it. On the way to church, she found a roadside patch of buttercups and wild roses. She made a wreath for her hat and put it on. Then she skipped merrily down the road, holding her pink-and-yellow-decorated head up proudly.

46

The little girls on the porch at church stared as Anne walked up. Her hat looked funny with pink and yellow flowers wound around it. They had heard about Anne. People said she had a terrible temper. She talked to the trees and flowers like a crazy girl. The little girls whispered to each other. Nobody tried to make friends with her.

Anne went in to her Sunday school class. The teacher was very strict. Every other little girl in the class had puffed sleeves. Anne was unhappy. She felt that life was not worth living without puffed sleeves.

Anne discarded her pretty wreath of flowers on the way home, since it had faded. When Anne reached Green Gables, she told Marilla all about Sunday school. She told her about the teacher, the prayers, and the lovely birch trees outside the window. She also told about the other children.

"There were nine girls in my class and they all had dresses with puffed sleeves. I tried to imagine my sleeves were puffed, but I couldn't. I could imagine they were puffed when I was alone in my bedroom, but it was awfully hard there with the other girls who had really truly puffs."

"You shouldn't have been thinking about your sleeves in Sunday school," Marilla scolded. "You should have been thinking about the lesson."

The one thing Anne forgot to tell Marilla was about putting the flowers on her hat.

The next Friday, Marilla came home all upset from Mrs. Lynde's.

"Anne, Mrs. Rachel says you went to church last Sunday with your hat rigged out with buttercups and wild roses. What on earth were you thinking?"

"Oh, I know pink and yellow don't look good on me," began Anne.

"Pink and yellow fiddlesticks! Putting flowers on your hat was ridiculous. Never mind the color. You looked just plain silly, Mrs. Rachel said. Everybody was looking at you. Of course, people thought I sent you dressed like that."

"I'm so sorry," said Anne, starting to cry. "I didn't think you'd mind. Lots of the other girls had artificial flowers on their hats. Some of them had little bouquets of artificial flowers on their dresses. The roses and buttercups were so sweet. They made my hat look pretty."

"Now, Anne. I just want you to act like other little girls and get along with folks," Marilla said. "Don't cry any more. I've got some good news for you. I'm going up to see Mrs. Barry this afternoon. I want to borrow a skirt pattern from her. If you like, you can come with me and meet Diana."

"Oh, Marilla—I'm frightened! What if she doesn't like me! It would be the most tragical disappointment of my life!"

"Now, don't get into a fluster," said Marilla. "Diana will like you well enough. It's her mother you've got to worry about. If she has heard about your outburst to Mrs. Lynde and going to church with buttercups on your hat, I don't know what she'll think. You must be polite and well behaved. If she doesn't like you, it won't matter how much Diana does."

They went over to the Barry's farm, Orchard Slope. Mrs. Barry answered the door. She introduced Anne to Diana.

Diana was sitting on the sofa, reading a book. She was a very pretty little girl, with black hair and rosy cheeks and a merry smile. Mrs. Barry sent the girls outside to play in the garden.

The Barry garden was a wilderness of flowers. If Anne had not been so worried about Diana liking her, she would have loved looking at all those flowers. But now Anne could only think about whether Diana would want to be her friend.

"Oh, Diana," asked Anne, "do you think you can like me a little, enough to be my dear friend?"

Diana laughed. Diana always laughed. "Why, I guess so," she said. "I'm glad you've come to live at Green Gables. It will be jolly to have somebody to play with."

"Will you promise to be my friend forever and ever?" Anne asked her.

"Well, I don't mind doing that," agreed Diana.

"Hold hands," said Anne. "I'll go first. I promise to be faithful to my dear friend, Diana Barry, forever. Now you say it and put my name in."

Diana repeated the promise. Then she said, "I believe I'm going to like you real well."

"Oh, Marilla," Anne said later, "I'm the happiest girl on Prince Edward Island. Diana and I are going to build a playhouse tomorrow. She's going to lend me a book to read and teach me a new song. She even knows a place where lilies grow."

"Well, all I hope is that you won't talk Diana to death," said Marilla.

Matthew made Anne's day even more perfect. He came home from the store and handed her a small package.

"I heard you say you liked chocolates, so I got you some," he said.

"Oh, Matthew!" said Anne eagerly. "Thank you! Can I give Diana half of them? They'll taste even better if I share them!"

"I will say this for the child," said Marilla when Anne had gone to her room, "she isn't stingy. It's only been three weeks since she came and I'm already getting fond of her. Now, don't you rub it in, Matthew Cuthbert."

CHAPTER FIVE

The Sunday School Picnic

Anne was late. She and Diana had been playing. Then she stopped in the yard to talk to Matthew. She talked and talked and talked. Inside the house, Marilla was getting upset.

"Anne Shirley, you come right in here this minute. Do you hear me?" the woman called.

Anne came running in with her eyes shining and her unbraided hair streaming. "Oh, Marilla," she said breathlessly, "there's going to be a Sunday school picnic next Wednesday in the field next to the Lake of Shining Waters. And there will be ice cream! I've never had ice cream before. And, oh, Marilla, can I go to it? Oh, please?"

"Just look at the clock, if you please, Anne. What time did I tell you to come in?"

"Two o'clock—but isn't it splendid about the picnic, Marilla? Please can I go? Oh, I've never been to a picnic—I've *dreamed* of picnics, but I've never—"

"I told you to come at two o'clock. And it's a quarter to three. I'd like to know why you didn't obey me, Anne."

"Why, I *meant* to, Marilla. But Diana and I were having so much fun playing. And then, of course, I had to tell Matthew about the picnic. Matthew is such a good listener. Please can I go?"

"Yes, of course you can go. You're in the Sunday school class, and all the little girls are going."

"But," said Anne, "Diana says that everybody must take a basket of things to eat. I don't know how to bake anything. I don't mind going to a picnic without puffed sleeves, but I'd feel awful if I had to go without a basket."

"Well, I'll bake you a basket."

"Oh, dear Marilla. You are so kind to me."

Anne was so happy that she threw her arms around Marilla and gave her a big kiss. Marilla wasn't much used to little girls' kisses.

"There, there, never mind your kissing nonsense," Marilla said. "I'd prefer that you do as you're told. As for cooking, I'll give you lessons one of these days. You know, you'll have to be careful when you're cooking. You can't daydream. You've got to keep your wits about you, or you'll burn the food. Or worse, you'll burn the house down."

"I'm sorry I was late. Diana and I *do* have such good times, Marilla," Anne said. She told Marilla all about their playhouse in the woods. It was in the middle of a ring of white birch trees. It had big stones, covered with moss, for seats, and boards from tree to tree for shelves. The girls used broken pieces of old dishes for their china. They kept a piece of fairy glass in a place of honor. The fairy glass was just an old prism from a lamp, but it was full of rainbows and magic to them.

For the rest of the week, Anne talked picnic and thought picnic and dreamed picnic. She talked about Diana's new dress for the picnic and about what she should take in her basket. Mostly, she talked about eating ice cream for the first time.

On Sunday, Anne and Marilla went to church. The minister announced the picnic from the pulpit. Anne grew more excited than ever.

Marilla wore her best brooch to church that day as usual, pinned to her dress. It had been her mother's and it was Marilla's most treasured possession. It was an old-fashioned oval with a border of very fine purple amethysts.

Anne loved the brooch. "Oh, Marilla, it's so beautiful! Amethysts are better than diamonds. I think they must be the souls of violets."

On Monday night, Marilla asked Anne, "Have you seen my amethyst brooch? I thought I stuck it in my pincushion when I came home from church yesterday, but I can't find it anywhere."

"I saw it this afternoon," said Anne slowly. "I saw it on the pincushion, so I went in to look at it. I pinned it on just to see how it would look. But I know I put it back."

"I'll go and have another look," said Marilla. She went to her room and searched everywhere. She could not find the brooch, and returned to the kitchen.

"Anne, the brooch is gone. Did you take it out and lose it?"

"No, I didn't," said Anne. "I never took the brooch out of your room."

"I don't believe you, Anne," Marilla said sharply. "Go to your room and stay there until you are ready to confess."

Marilla told Matthew the story the next morning. Matthew was puzzled, but he had faith in Anne.

"You're sure it didn't fall down behind the dresser?" he asked.

"I've looked in every crack and cranny," was Marilla's positive answer. "The brooch is gone and she lied about it."

Anne stayed in her room all day. Marilla brought up her meals on a tray. "You'll stay in this room until you confess, Anne," she said firmly that night at bedtime.

"But the picnic is tomorrow, Marilla," cried Anne. "You won't keep me from going to that, will you?"

"You're not going to the picnic or anywhere else until you've confessed, Anne," Marilla said. She shut the door as she left.

On Wednesday morning, Marilla took Anne's breakfast up to her.

63

"Marilla, I'm ready to confess," Anne said.

"Let me hear what you have to say then, Anne."

"I took the brooch," said Anne. "I took it just like you said. I didn't mean to, but it was so beautiful, Marilla. I took it to our playhouse, to pretend I was a grand lady. When I was going over the bridge across the Lake of Shining Waters, it just slipped through my fingers—and went down—down—down, all purply-sparkling, and sank forevermore beneath the water. And that's the best I can do at confessing and I know I'll have to be punished. Please do it quickly, because I'd like to go to the picnic with nothing on my mind."

"Picnic! You'll go to no picnic today, Anne Shirley! That shall be your punishment."

"Not go to the picnic!" Anne cried. "You promised! Oh, Marilla, that's why I confessed. Please, please, let me go to the picnic. Think of the ice cream!"

"Don't beg, Anne. You are not going to the picnic and that's final."

Anne flung herself on the bed, crying in despair.

But Marilla would not be moved by the tears, and went back down to the kitchen, very upset. She hated to think that Anne would lie to her.

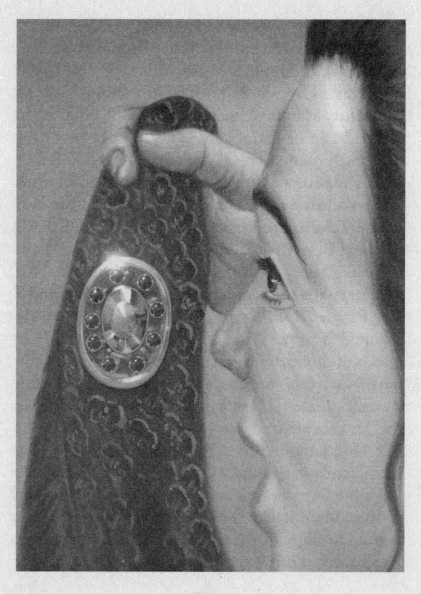

After she washed the noon dishes, Marilla remembered that she had to mend her good black shawl. She had noticed a small tear in it on Monday. The shawl was in her trunk. Marilla lifted it out and saw something sparkling in the sunlight. Marilla gasped. It was the amethyst brooch, caught on a thread of the shawl!

"Goodness," said Marilla. "Here's my brooch. Why did Anne say she lost it? I remember now that when I took off my shawl Monday, I laid it on the dresser for a minute. I suppose the brooch got caught in it somehow."

Marilla went straight to Anne's room. "Anne Shirley," said Marilla, "I just found my brooch hanging on my black shawl. I want to know why you confessed."

"You said you'd keep me here until I confessed," said Anne wearily, "so I decided to confess so I could go to the picnic."

Marilla had to laugh in spite of herself. But she felt guilty, too. "Anne, it wasn't right for you to confess to something you didn't do, but I drove you to it. So if you'll forgive me, I'll forgive you. And now get ready for the picnic. I'll fill a basket for you."

Anne came home from the picnic tired and happy. "Oh, Marilla, I've had a perfectly wonderful time. We went for boat rides on the Lake of Shining Waters. And we had the ice cream. It was divine!"

That evening Marilla told Matthew, "There's one thing certain, things will never be dull with Anne around!"

CHAPTER SIX

Troubles for Anne

When Anne went off to start school on the first day of September, Marilla was worried. Would Anne get along with the other children? How would she ever hold her tongue during lessons? But things went more smoothly than Marilla thought they would. Anne liked school, made lots of friends, and got along just fine.

Every day, Anne and Diana walked to school together. They had a wonderful time as they walked under the red and gold maple trees and around by the Lake of Shining Waters.

Three weeks into the school year, Anne hadn't gotten into any trouble at all.

One morning as they walked to school, Diana told Anne that Gilbert Blythe would be back in school that day. Gilbert had been helping on his uncle's farm during the summer. He had just gotten back to Avonlea. Diana said Gilbert was handsome and liked to tease the girls. He was a little older than Anne and Diana. He was smart and was used to being the best in his class. Anne liked being best in the class, too.

When they sat down in the schoolroom, Anne looked across the aisle. There was Gilbert Blythe, a tall boy with curly brown hair and hazel eyes. He winked at her. She quickly turned away.

That afternoon, while the teacher, Mr. Phillips, was busy at the back of the classroom, Gilbert tried to get Anne's attention. He winked at her again. She ignored him. Gilbert wasn't used to being ignored. Most of the girls liked it when he teased and flirted.

"She *should* look at me, this redheaded girl with the big eyes. What is the matter with this Anne Shirley girl?" he thought. He reached across the aisle and picked up the end of Anne's long red braid. He whispered so everyone could hear, "Carrots! Carrots!"

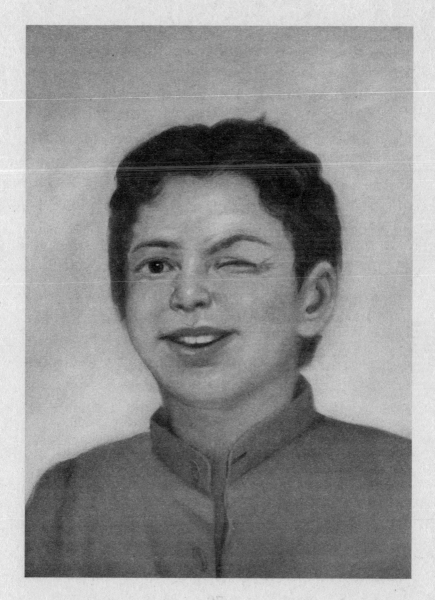

71

Anne didn't ignore him anymore. She jumped up and burst into angry tears. "You mean boy! How dare you!" And then—*thwack!* Anne hit Gilbert over the head with her slate. The slate cracked, but Gilbert wasn't hurt.

Mr. Phillips rushed to see what was going on. He made Anne stand in the corner for the rest of the day. She did not cry or hang her head. She was too angry to cry. She promised herself that she would never, ever talk to Gilbert again. She would never even look at him.

When school was dismissed, Gilbert met her by the schoolhouse door.

"I'm sorry I made fun of your hair, Anne," he said. "Honest I am. Don't be mad."

Anne walked past him like she didn't even see him.

The very next day, Anne got in trouble again.

Mr. Phillips went to the nearest farm for lunch every day. That day, when he left for lunch, he told the children to be back in their seats when he returned. He said that anyone who was late would be punished. During lunch recess, all the children played in the woods behind the schoolhouse. When the bell rang, the girls ran back quickly.

They sat down without a second to spare. The boys were playing a little farther away. They also ran toward the schoolhouse. Anne, who had been daydreaming at the very farthest part of the woods, was last. She ran fast and caught up to the boys, just as they got to the door of the schoolhouse. The teacher was waiting for them. He didn't want to bother with punishing all of the latecomers, so he decided to punish just Anne to make his point.

"Anne Shirley, since you seem to like the boys so much, you will sit with Gilbert this afternoon," the teacher said. "Did you hear what I said, Anne? Obey me at once!"

Anne felt angry and humiliated. It was so unfair! She walked across the aisle and sat down beside Gilbert. She buried her face in her arms on the desk. It was bad enough to be the only one punished when they were all guilty. It was worse to have to sit with a boy. Worst of all, that boy was Gilbert!

When school let out, Anne went to her desk and took everything out. Her mind was made up. She would not go to back to school—ever again. She told Marilla so when she got home.

"Nonsense," said Marilla.

"I'm not going back, Marilla." Anne shook her head. "I'll learn my lessons at home. I will not go back to school."

Anne was so stubborn about this that Marilla didn't know what to do with her. She decided to go to Mrs. Rachel Lynde for advice.

"I heard about Anne's fuss at school," Mrs. Lynde told Marilla.

"I don't know what to do with her," Marilla replied. "She says she won't go back to school. What should I do, Rachel?"

"Well, I think Mr. Phillips was wrong, but I wouldn't tell the child that. He should have punished all of them that were late, not just Anne. If I were you, I would let her stay home for a while. If you force her to go now while she's mad, she might get in even more trouble. She will soon wonder what she's missing and decide to go back."

Marilla took Mrs. Lynde's advice. Anne learned her lessons at home, did her chores, and played with Diana. Diana tried to get Anne to forgive Gilbert Blythe, but this was the one thing that Anne would not do for her friend.

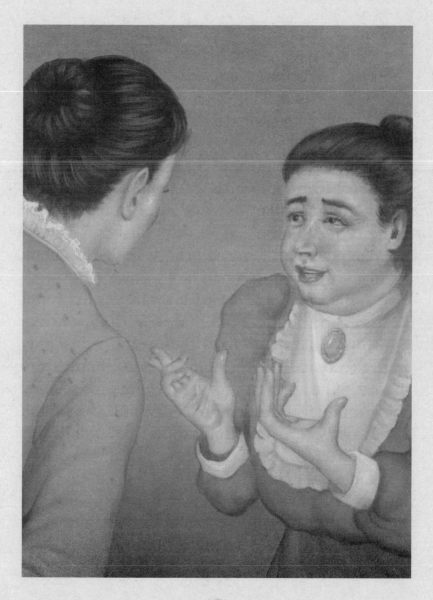

One Saturday in October, Marilla told Anne she could invite Diana for tea.

"Oh, Marilla!" Anne said. "How perfectly lovely!"

"I have to go to my ladies' club meeting," Marilla said. "Use the old brown tea set. And you can have some of the cookies. There's some raspberry cordial on the second shelf of the sitting room closet, too. You and Diana can have some of it, if you like."

When Diana arrived, the two girls shook hands like grownups do. They went up to Anne's east gable room, and sat with their toes in proper position and chatted. They were *ever* so polite to each other. After a while, they went out to play in the orchard. All afternoon, they ate apples and talked. The girls had a very good time. Diana told Anne all the school news. When she talked about Gilbert, Anne jumped up and said, "Let's go in now."

Anne went to the sitting room to get the raspberry cordial. She looked on the second shelf of the closet like Marilla had told her. The raspberry cordial wasn't there. She looked on the top shelf. There it was! She put it on a tray with a tall glass.

"Please help yourself, Diana," she said politely. "I don't want any right now. I'm still full from all the apples."

Diana poured herself a glassful and took a sip. "That's awfully nice raspberry cordial, Anne," she said.

"I'm real glad you like it. Take as much as you want."

Diana drank a second glassful of cordial, and then a third. Anne just chattered on and on and on. "Why, Diana, what is the matter?" Anne asked at last.

Diana stood up, then staggered. She sat down again, holding her head.

"I'm awful sick," she said. "I must go right home. I'm awful dizzy."

Anne walked Diana to the Barry's fence. Then she went back to Green Gables and got tea ready for Matthew.

The next afternoon, Anne came home crying. "Mrs. Barry said that I got Diana drunk Saturday!" she said. "She's never going to let Diana play with me again. Oh, Marilla!"

Marilla was amazed. "Got Diana drunk? What did you give her?"

"Just raspberry cordial," cried Anne. "I didn't think it would get people drunk, not even if they drank three glasses."

Marilla went to the sitting room closet. There on the shelf was her homemade currant wine. Then she remembered putting the raspberry cordial down in the cellar. It was not in the closet like she had told Anne.

"Anne, you gave Diana currant wine instead of raspberry cordial. Didn't you know the difference?"

"I never tasted it," wailed Anne. "Diana got awfully sick and had to go home. Mrs. Barry said that she was simply flat drunk. She thinks I did it on purpose."

Marilla went to Mrs. Barry to set things straight, but Mrs. Barry didn't believe her. She said Diana couldn't play with Anne ever again. Poor Anne cried herself to sleep that night.

Anne was very sad. She moped around the house all day. The next Monday she surprised Marilla. She said that she was going back to school. She would do her best to be a good student. It was better than sitting home all alone, with no friend to play with.

The children were all happy to see Anne. They had missed her. After lunch, Gilbert tried to give her an apple, but she wouldn't touch it.

Anne worked very hard on her lessons. Gilbert would not be best in the class if she could help it. Gilbert thought it was all in fun, but for Anne it was war. One day Gilbert would lead in spelling, but the next day Anne would pull ahead. One morning Gilbert would make the best grade in arithmetic, but the next day Anne would win the prize. By the end of the term, both Anne and Gilbert were promoted to the next grade. They started studying harder subjects, like Latin and geometry.

CHAPTER SEVEN

Anne to the Rescue

In January, the Premier of Canada came to Prince Edward Island to give a speech in Charlottetown, thirty miles from Avonlea. Almost all of the adults went to hear him speak. Marilla rode with Mrs. Lynde and the Barrys. Anne and Matthew stayed behind at Green Gables and had the cheerful kitchen all to themselves.

A bright fire glowed in the old fashioned stove and blue-white frost shone on the windowpanes. Matthew was nodding off over his newspaper. Anne sat at the table, studying her lessons.

"Matthew, did you ever study geometry when you went to school?" asked Anne.

"Well now, no, I didn't," said Matthew.

"I wish you had," sighed Anne. "Then you'd understand how hard it is for me. It is casting a cloud over my whole life. I'm such a dunce at it."

"Well now, I dunno," said Matthew quietly. "I guess you're all right at anything. The teacher told me last week in Blair's store that you're the smartest student in school."

"Well, I suppose I must finish up my lessons. And then I'll run down to the cellar and get some apples. Matthew, wouldn't you like some apples?"

Just as Anne came up from the cellar, the back door flew open. Diana rushed in, wide-eyed and out of breath. She was shivering from the cold, with just a thin shawl wrapped around her.

"Oh, Anne, do come quick," begged Diana. "Minnie May has croup. Father and Mother are gone. There's nobody to go for the doctor. Minnie May is awful bad. Oh, Anne, I'm so scared!"

Matthew didn't say a word. Quickly he put on his coat and went to hitch up the buggy. He headed to town to get the doctor.

Diana said, "Oh, Anne, he won't find a doctor. So many people have gone to the speech!" And Diana started to sob.

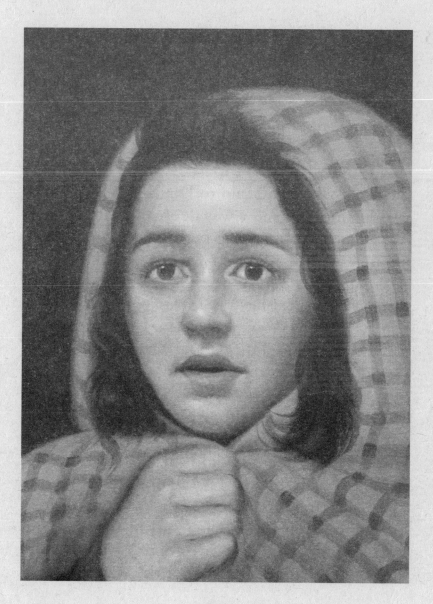

87

"Don't cry, Diana," said Anne. "I know exactly what to do for croup. You forget I took care of Mrs. Thomas's and Mrs. Hammond's children. They always had the croup. I'll just get the medicine. You might not have any at your house."

Anne went to the pantry and pulled out a small brown bottle of ipecac. Then she quickly put her coat on and said to Diana, "Let's go."

Outside, the snow was deep and the night air was clear and frosty. The two girls ran all the way, hand in hand, to the Barry house.

Diana's sister, Minnie May, age three, was really very sick. She was feverish and she could hardly breathe. Young Mary Joe, the babysitter, was helpless and didn't know what to do.

Anne quickly went to work.

"Minnie May has got croup, all right, but I've seen it worse," she said. She told Mary Joe to put wood in the stove and had Diana boil water in the kettle. The steam would make it easier for Minnie May to breathe. Anne undressed Minnie May, tucked her into bed, and gave her a dose of medicine. Anne and Diana stayed up all night, taking care of the little girl. Anne gave her more doses of medicine. Diana kept the water boiling.

Matthew had to go three towns away to find a doctor. Everyone, it seemed, was at the Premier's speech. It was three o'clock in the morning before he finally got to the Barry's with the doctor. By then, Minnie May was much better. She was asleep and her breathing was fine.

When the Barrys got home, the doctor told them that Anne had saved Minnie May's life.

"That little redheaded girl is as smart as they come," he said to Mrs. Barry. "I tell you, she saved that baby's life. It would have been too late by the time I got here. She has skills and sense way beyond her age. I never saw anything like her."

Anne and Matthew made their way home through the frosty sunrise. Anne was very tired, but she talked the whole way. She told Matthew that she really wanted to go to school that day. She was afraid that she would get behind the others, especially Gilbert, if she didn't go. But she was just too tired. She went to bed and slept most of the day. When she got up, it was late in the afternoon. She was very hungry and went right down to the kitchen. Marilla fixed Anne some dinner. Then she told her that Mrs. Barry had come over while Anne was sleeping.

"Mrs. Barry says you saved Minnie May's life. She is very sorry she was mean to you. She wants you to forgive her and be good friends with Diana again. You can go visit them right now, if you like."

Anne ran right over and had a grand visit with the Barrys. She and Diana had tea. They even made taffy. Mrs. Barry was very sorry and she was extra nice to Anne. Best of all, Anne had her best friend back!

CHAPTER EIGHT

A New Flavor for Cake

On the last day of the school term, the students said good-bye to their teacher. Mr. Phillips was not coming back for the next school year.

It was also a time of hellos in Avonlea. A new minister and his wife had arrived—Reverend and Mrs. Allan, a very nice young couple. The town liked them at once. Anne fell in love with Mrs. Allan and knew they would be the best of friends.

"I suppose we must have Mr. and Mrs. Allan up to tea someday soon," said Marilla one day. "Next Wednesday would be a good time. But don't say a word to Matthew about it. He is so shy, the thought of a new minister's wife will frighten him to death."

"Oh, Marilla," Anne begged, "will you let me make a cake? I'd love to do something for Mrs. Allan. You know I can make a pretty good cake now."

"You can make a layer cake," promised Marilla.

Having the minister and his wife to tea was a serious project. Anne was so excited. She talked it all over with Diana on Tuesday as they sat outside in the twilight.

"Everything is ready, Diana, except my cake. I'll make that in the morning. We're going to have two kinds of jelly, and lemon pie, and cherry pie, and three kinds of cookies, and fruit cake and layer cake. Oh, Diana, what if my cake doesn't turn out right!" Anne remembered how many mistakes she had made while learning to cook.

"It'll be good, I know it will," assured Diana, who was a very comfortable sort of friend.

Wednesday morning, Anne got up at sunrise. She had a bad cold from staying out in the damp air with Diana the night before. But nothing less than pneumonia could keep her out of the kitchen today! After breakfast she carefully made her cake. It came out of the oven light and feathery. Anne put it together with layers of ruby jelly.

The tea was a big success. Even shy Matthew enjoyed himself. At last Anne passed out pieces of her layer cake. Mrs. Allan helped herself to a big piece. So did the minister and Marilla. Mrs. Allan took a bite and got a very strange look on her face. She didn't say anything, though. She didn't want to hurt Anne's feelings.

Marilla tasted the cake. "Anne Shirley!" she said. "What did you put into this cake?"

"Only what the recipe said, Marilla," cried Anne. "Oh, isn't it all right?"

"It's awful, Anne. Taste it yourself. What flavoring did you use?"

"Vanilla," said Anne, her face turning red. "Only vanilla."

"Go and bring me the bottle of vanilla you used."

Anne ran to the pantry. She returned with a bottle labeled "Best Vanilla." Marilla took it, uncorked it, and smelled it.

"Mercy, Anne, this is liniment. I broke the medicine bottle last week and poured what was left into an old empty vanilla bottle. I should have warned you, but for pity's sake, couldn't you smell it?"

Anne burst into tears. "I couldn't! I have such a cold I can't smell anything!" She ran sobbing to her room. Mrs. Allan followed her quietly.

"My dear, don't cry," she said. "Why, it's all just a funny mistake that anybody could make."

"Oh, no, it takes me to make mistakes like this," said Anne sadly. "And I wanted that cake to be so nice for you, Mrs. Allan."

"Yes, I know, dear. I appreciate the thought very much. Now, don't cry any more. Come show me your flower garden. I love flowers."

No one said anything more about the liniment cake. After the guests left, Anne sighed, "Marilla, isn't it nice to think that tomorrow is a new day with no mistakes in it yet?"

Toward the end of summer, Anne came running home to Green Gables.

"Marilla! Mrs. Allan invited me to tea at the minister's house tomorrow! She is going to invite each of the girls in our Sunday school class one at a time!"

Anne thought that the next morning would never come. She worried that it might rain and spoil her plans. When she woke up, sunshine was pouring in her window. It was a beautiful morning and a perfect day for a tea.

"Oh, Marilla," Anne said. "I feel so good. I could be good every day if I was invited out to tea. Marilla, but what if I don't act properly? I don't know much about good manners. I'm afraid I'll do something silly."

"Just do what you think will be nicest for Mrs. Allan," said Marilla wisely. "If you think about her instead of yourself, you'll get along fine."

Anne went to the tea and used her very best manners. She told Marilla all about it later.

"Oh, Marilla, I've had a most wonderful time. When I got there, Mrs. Allan met me at the door. She was dressed in a pale pink dress with lace and pearls. She looked like an angel. Mrs. Allan is such a good person. I just love her. I wish I could be good. We had an elegant tea, and I think I minded my manners just fine. Mrs. Allan and I had a heart-to-heart talk. I told her all about living with Mrs. Thomas and Mrs. Hammond and all the children I took care of. I told her

about coming to Green Gables and my troubles over geometry. And would you believe it, Marilla? Mrs. Allan told me she was a dunce at geometry, too. I told her all about Diana and our playhouse. Mrs. Lynde stopped by just before I left. She said the trustees have hired a new teacher and it's a lady. Her name is Miss Muriel Stacy. Isn't that a romantic name? I think it will be wonderful to have a lady teacher. I don't see how I'm going to live through the two weeks before school begins. I can hardly wait!"

CHAPTER NINE

A Matter of Honor
and Puffed Sleeves

Anne was overdue for trouble. It had been more than a month since she put liniment in the cake. She had made some little mistakes since then, but nothing that amounted to much.

Just before school opened, Diana Barry gave a party for all the girls in the class. They had a lovely tea and then went outside to play in the garden. After a while they got bored, started looking for mischief, and decided to play "Daring." Daring, which had been started by the boys, was the most popular game in town. It was the cause of silliness all over Avonlea.

First, Carrie Sloane dared Ruby Gillis to climb the huge old willow tree. Ruby scampered up it, even though it had caterpillars in all the branches. Then Josie Pye dared Jane Andrews to hop around the garden on one foot without stopping. Jane only got halfway around and had to stop. Josie teased Jane about not winning the dare. Then Anne dared Josie to walk the top of the board fence. Josie did it easily. Next, Josie dared Anne to walk the ridgepole on top of the Barry's kitchen roof. It was a long way off the ground. The other girls told Anne not to do it. They were afraid she would get hurt.

Anne was scared, but she said she had to do it. "My honor is at stake," Anne told them. "I will walk that ridgepole or die trying."

She walked toward the house. There was a ladder leaning against the kitchen roof. Anne climbed up to the roof and balanced herself on the ridgepole. She took several careful steps, but then she lost her balance. She slid down the roof and crashed into the vines below.

The girls shrieked and rushed to Anne. She was lying still and limp in the vines. Her face was very white.

Mrs. Barry came running out of the house. She heard the clatter and wanted to know what had happened. Anne tried to get up, but fell down with a cry of pain.

"What's the matter? Where have you hurt yourself?" asked Mrs. Barry.

"My ankle," said Anne. "Oh, Diana, please go find your father and ask him to take me home."

Mr. Barry carried Anne home in his arms. She was as limp as a rag doll. Mrs. Barry walked beside him. The little girls came after. Marilla was scared when she saw them coming and rushed to meet them.

"Mr. Barry, what happened to her?" Marilla cried out.

"Don't be scared, Marilla," Anne lifted her head and answered. "I fell off the roof. I think I sprained my ankle."

"Bring her in here, Mr. Barry, and lay her on the sofa," Marilla said. "Mercy me, she's fainted!"

It was true. Anne had fainted from the pain.

Matthew went for the doctor, who came and examined Anne. He told them that her ankle was broken. That night, Marilla tucked a very sorry little girl into bed.

"Don't be cross with me, Marilla. It hurt dreadfully to have my ankle set. I'll be laid up for six or seven weeks and I'll miss the first day of school with the new lady teacher. And Gil—I mean—everybody will get ahead of me in class."

"There, there, I'm not angry," said Marilla. "You're an unlucky child, there's no doubt about that. Here now, try and eat some supper."

Anne had lots of visitors in the seven weeks that followed.

"Everybody has been so kind, Marilla," sighed Anne. It was the first day she could walk again. "There's only one good thing about being hurt. You find out how many friends you have." Mrs. Allan had visited her several times and Diana came every day. Anne told Marilla all the news from school she had learned—and all about Miss Stacy, the new teacher with curly hair and puffed sleeves. As usual, Anne talked and talked and talked.

"Well, one thing is plain, Anne," said Marilla. "Your fall off the Barry roof hasn't injured your tongue at all."

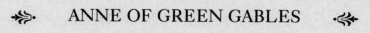

One cold December evening, Matthew watched Anne and her friends playing. Anne stood in the middle of the group. Matthew saw that somehow she looked different from the other girls. He couldn't say exactly how. Anne was prettier, but that was not the difference. There was something else, but what was it? It bothered Matthew all evening. He knew he could not ask Marilla.

Matthew finally figured it out for himself. Anne was not *dressed* like the other girls! Marilla made her plain dresses with tight sleeves. That was the difference! All the other girls had puffed sleeves. Their dresses were in prettier colors, too. He wondered why Marilla always kept Anne dressed so plainly. Of course, it must be all right. Marilla knew best and Marilla was bringing her up.

Still, Matthew thought it might be all right if Anne had just one pretty dress. That wouldn't be spoiling her too much, would it? Marilla wouldn't mind that, would she? A pretty dress like Diana Barry always wore. He decided that he would give her one. Christmas was only two weeks away. A pretty new dress would be the very thing for a present!

The next evening, Matthew went to town to buy a dress. Matthew hated shopping, even for farm supplies. He was afraid of store clerks, especially lady store clerks. When he got into the store that evening and saw a lady working at the counter, he felt very, very shy. He was afraid to ask her for help picking out a dress, so he asked about rakes and seeds instead. Matthew got so confused that he went home with twenty pounds of brown sugar, but no dress.

He needed a woman's help to solve the problem, Matthew decided. He couldn't ask Marilla because she might get upset. She thought Anne's plain dresses were just fine. He went to see Mrs. Lynde and she was happy to take over. She bought some nice brown fabric and made Anne a pretty dress with puffed sleeves and lace trim. Mrs. Lynde brought it over to Matthew on Christmas Eve.

Anne ran downstairs on Christmas morning. "Merry Christmas, Marilla! Merry Christmas, Matthew! Isn't it a lovely Christmas?"

Then Anne saw Matthew. He was holding out a dress to Anne.

"Oh, Matthew! Is it for me?" Anne whispered.

She looked at the dress quietly. Oh, how pretty it was! It had a frilly skirt and a little ruffle of lace at the neck. But the sleeves—they were too beautiful! Big puffed sleeves with bows of brown silk ribbon! Tears welled up in her gray eyes.

"That's a Christmas present for you, Anne," said Matthew shyly. "Why, Anne, don't you like it? Well now, well now."

"*Like* it! Oh, Matthew!" Anne said through her tears as she clasped her hands. "Matthew, it's perfectly exquisite. Oh, I can never thank you enough. Look at those sleeves! Oh, it seems to me this must be a happy dream."

Anne got to wear her new dress to the Christmas program at school that evening. She felt so pretty and she was so proud of her puffed sleeves. It was the best Christmas she had ever had.

That night Marilla and Matthew sat by the kitchen fire after Anne had gone to bed.

"Well now, I guess our Anne had a good Christmas," said Matthew proudly.

"Yes, she did," admitted Marilla. "She did well in the Christmas program. And she looked real pretty in her dress, too."

"Well now," Matthew went on, "she's starting to grow up. She'll be thirteen in March. She'll need something more than Avonlea school one of these days."

"There's time enough to think of that," said Marilla. "I guess we should send her to Queen's Academy after a spell. But not for a year or two yet."

"Well now, it won't hurt to start thinking about it," said Matthew.

CHAPTER TEN

More Trouble for Anne

One evening in late April, Marilla was walking home from a church meeting. Winter was over and spring was creeping across Avonlea. Marilla looked forward to coming home to a warm fire. She thought about how nice it would be to hear about Anne's day.

But when she got home, there was no fire and no sign of Anne. Marilla was a little angry. She started a fire. She would give Anne a talking to when she got home. When Anne did not come in time for tea, Marilla got *very* angry.

"She's off playing with Diana or writing stories," she told Matthew. "Anne can be such a scatterbrain! I can't trust her to do her chores."

"Well now, I dunno," said Matthew. "Perhaps you're judging her too hasty, Marilla. Maybe it can all be explained."

Anne did not appear for supper, either. Marilla's anger turned to worry. When she went to Anne's room to find a candle, she found Anne instead, lying on the bed.

"Anne, you had me worried. Have you been asleep? Are you sick?" asked Marilla.

Anne hid under her pillows. "No. Marilla, go away and don't look at me. I can never go anywhere again. Please don't look at me."

"Anne Shirley, what is the matter with you? Get up this minute and tell me. What is it?"

"Look at my hair, Marilla," Anne whispered.

Marilla lifted her candle and looked at Anne's hair. "Anne Shirley, what have you done? Why, it's green!"

"Yes, it's green," moaned Anne. "I thought nothing could be as bad as red hair. But now I know. It's ten times worse to have green hair!"

"You haven't been in any trouble for over two months," Marilla said. "It was *time* for something to happen. Now tell me what you did."

"I dyed it," said Anne. "I just wanted to get rid of my red hair."

"But why green?" said Marilla. "At least you could have dyed it a pretty color."

"I didn't *mean* to dye it green, Marilla," Anne explained. "The peddler said it would turn my hair a beautiful black. He was such a nice man. He told me all about his family and how poor they are. I wanted to help him so I bought the dye. He said it would turn any hair a beautiful black and wouldn't wash off. So I put it on. I followed all the directions. I used the whole bottle! Oh, Marilla, I've been sorry ever since."

The peddler was telling the truth. The dye wouldn't wash off. For a week, Anne shampooed her hair every day. She scrubbed and scrubbed and scrubbed. It didn't change the color one bit. It was still green. They finally decided that the only way to fix it was to cut it off.

"Please cut it off at once, Marilla," said Anne, "and have it over. Oh, how my heart is broken."

Marilla cut Anne's hair very, very short. The haircut looked awful. Anne said she would never look into a mirror again. On Monday at school, Josie Pye called her a scarecrow.

When Anne came home that day, Marilla was resting. She had a bad headache. Anne told her all about her day at school. She even told her what Josie said. Then Anne asked, "Am I talking too much, Marilla? Does it hurt your head?"

"My head is better now. It was bad this afternoon, though. These headaches of mine are getting worse and worse. I'll have to see a doctor about them. As for your chatter, I don't mind it." That was Marilla's way of saying that she liked to hear Anne talk about her day.

Summer came again to Avonlea and the afternoons were filled with daydreams, story-telling, and adventures. Diana and Anne were playing by Barry's Pond with their friends Jane and Ruby. They were acting out a romantic fairy tale they had read in school. In the story, the princess dies. Her body is placed in a small boat and floated across a lake. Anne was going to play the princess. She would lie down in the bottom of the rowboat and float across the pond. The girls would wait for her on the other side.

The girls put an old black shawl in the bottom of the boat. Anne lay down on it. Then they covered her with a scarf and put an iris in her folded hands. They thought she looked just like the dead princess in the story. The girls pushed the boat off from the bank, but it scraped a sharp piece of metal along the way. Without knowing this, Diana, Ruby, and Jane ran off so they could meet the boat on the other side of the pond.

The boat drifted slowly across the large pond. For a few minutes, Anne had fun playing the dead princess. Then the boat began to leak. The metal piece on the bank had scraped a hole in the bottom. Water poured in. The boat was sinking. Where were the oars? Left behind at the landing!

There was just one chance! Ahead was the bridge. Its bridge pilings were old tree trunks with knots and branch stubs on them. As the boat floated close to the pilings, Anne grabbed one, scrambled up, and clung to the slippery stubs.

The boat floated under the bridge—and then sank. The girls saw the boat sink and thought Anne had drowned! They ran fast to get help. Anne was left clinging to the bridge pile. It was not romantic in the least.

Anne held on for dear life. She had no way to get off. Her hands started to cramp. It seemed like she had been there for hours. Why didn't somebody come? Where had the girls gone? Surely they would go for help! Suppose nobody ever came! Anne looked at the cold water swirling below her. Her imagination thought up all kinds of horrible things. She was afraid of falling into the cold green water.

Just when she was about to give up hope, Gilbert Blythe came rowing another boat from the other side of the pond. He came under the bridge and saw Anne on the pile.

"Anne Shirley! How on earth did you get there?" he exclaimed.

Gilbert stretched out his hand to help her. She took his hand and scrambled into the boat. Anne was dripping wet and scared, but she still hated Gilbert. She tried to be dignified.

"We were playing," Anne said, without looking at him. "The boat sank, and I climbed out onto the bridge pile. I'm sure the girls went for help. Will you please row me to the landing?" Anne was very embarrassed.

Gilbert rowed to the landing and Anne jumped out of the boat.

"Thank you," she said stiffly. She turned and walked away without another word.

"Come on, Anne," Gilbert called after her, "I'm sorry I made fun of your hair that time. It was so long ago. Can't we be friends?"

For a moment, Anne thought about it. Then the old anger came back. "No," she said. "I will never be friends with you, Gilbert, and I don't want to be!"

On the walk back she met her worried friends who were thrilled to see her alive and well. They had been trying to find help, but no one was around. How romantic they thought it was that Gilbert had rescued Anne! Anne did not want to hear that word "romantic" again.

Marilla and Matthew were upset when they heard the story.

"Will you ever have any sense, Anne?" said Marilla.

"Well, Marilla," said Anne, "I've learned a new lesson today. Every time I make a mistake, I learn something new. The amethyst brooch cured me of meddling with other people's things. The liniment cake taught me not to be careless when I'm cooking. Dyeing my hair cured me of vanity. Today's mistake has cured me of being too romantic. So you can see I'm really learning a lot by making mistakes, Marilla."

"I sure hope so," said Marilla.

But Matthew whispered, "A little romance is a good thing. Keep a little of it, Anne, keep a little of it."

CHAPTER ELEVEN

The Queen's Class Is Formed

One dark November evening, well into the next school year, Marilla put down her knitting and looked at Anne. Lost in her dreams, Anne was reading by the fire.

"Anne," said Marilla, "your teacher, Miss Stacy, was here this afternoon."

"Was she? Oh, I'm so sorry I wasn't here. What did she want?"

"She came to talk to me about you."

"About me?" Anne looked scared. Then she got red. "Oh, I know what she came to say. I meant to tell you, Marilla, honestly I did, but I forgot. Miss Stacy caught me reading a novel in school

133

yesterday afternoon when I should have been studying my history. Jane lent it to me. I was reading it at lunchtime. I just couldn't put it down when we went back in. I spread the history open on my desk and then hid the novel on my lap. Then Miss Stacy caught me. I felt so ashamed. She took the novel away and didn't say a word about it until recess. She told me it was wrong to waste my study time and it was wrong to try to fool her. I told her how sorry I was and she forgave me. I didn't think she'd come to tell you about it."

"Miss Stacy didn't say a word about any novel, Anne. It's your guilty conscience that's bothering you. You have no business to be taking storybooks to school. You read too many novels anyhow. When I was a girl, I wasn't allowed to look at a novel. Now," Marilla went on, "do you want to know what Miss Stacy told me?"

"Oh, please tell me, Marilla!" Anne said.

"Well, Miss Stacy wants to organize a special class. She'll help the class study for the entrance exam into Queen's Academy. She will give extra lessons for an hour after school. She came to ask Matthew and me if we would like to have you join the class. We've planned for you to go to Queen's. We'll pay your way. What do you think, Anne? Would you like to go to Queen's to be a teacher?"

"Oh, Marilla!" Anne exclaimed. "I'd love to be a teacher."

The Queen's class soon started. Gilbert Blythe, Anne, Ruby Gillis, Jane Andrews, Josie Pye, Charlie Sloane, and Moody MacPherson joined it. Diana did not. Her parents weren't going to send her to Queen's. It broke Anne's heart to be separated from her dear friend.

Anne and Gilbert were still rivals. The rest of the class knew that Anne and Gilbert were the smartest. They never even tried to compete with them. Since the day by the pond, Gilbert had ignored Anne. Anne didn't like being ignored. She tried to tell herself that she did not care, but deep down she did. And now it was too late.

The winter passed. The Queen's class studied very hard. Almost before Anne realized it, spring had come again to Green Gables. All the world was in bloom once more.

The Queen's class looked out the schoolroom windows. It was hard to study when they could see the other children playing outside. Even Anne

and Gilbert grew tired of their studies. Everyone was glad when the school term ended and vacation began.

When Anne got home that night she locked all her textbooks away in an old trunk in the attic.

"I'm not going to look at a schoolbook during vacation," she told Marilla. "I've studied hard all term. I'm going to have lots of fun playing this summer. I'm fourteen now, and this might be the last summer I'll be a little girl."

Mrs. Rachel Lynde came up to Green Gables the next afternoon. She wanted to know why Marilla had not been at the church ladies' meeting on Thursday.

"Matthew had a bad spell with his heart Thursday," Marilla told her. "I didn't want to leave him. He's all right again now. He just can't do any very heavy work. You might as well tell Matthew not to breathe as not to work. Come in, Rachel. You'll stay for tea?"

Mrs. Rachel and Marilla sat in the parlor while Anne got the tea and made hot biscuits. Her biscuits were light and fluffy enough even to please Mrs. Rachel, who was very fussy about such things.

"Your Anne has turned out just fine," Mrs. Rachel said to Marilla. "She must be a great help to you."

"She is," said Marilla. "She's real steady and reliable now."

"I didn't think she'd turn out so well the first day I met her. That was three whole years ago," said Mrs. Rachel. "It's wonderful to see how she's grown. She's so smart and such a real pretty girl, too."

CHAPTER TWELVE

Anne Grows Up

The summer was a golden one for Anne. She walked, rowed, picked berries, and dreamed to her heart's content. When September came, she was ready for school once more. She happily got her books from the attic—even geometry.

Miss Stacy came back to Avonlea school. All of her students were eager to get back to their lessons. The Queen's class was especially eager. At the end of this year, they had to take the exam, known as "The Entrance." If they passed the test, they could go to study at Queen's. But it was a hard test and all of them worried about failing. Anne dreaded failing—and Gilbert passing!

The winter passed quickly. Anne was very busy and having a jolly time. Schoolwork was interesting, for Miss Stacy led her class to think and explore and discover for themselves. Fresh new worlds opened out before Anne's eyes.

One day, Marilla and Anne were standing side by side. Marilla was surprised to see that Anne was taller than she was. Where had her little girl gone? The child she had learned to love had vanished somehow. Now there was a tall girl of fifteen in her place.

That night, while Anne was out with Diana, Marilla was crying. Matthew came in and asked her what was wrong.

"I was thinking about Anne," she explained. "She'll go away to Queen's next school year. She's grown up so fast! I'll miss her terribly."

"She'll be able to come home often," said Matthew gently.

"It won't be the same thing as having her here all the time," sighed Marilla.

Anne not only grew taller. She got quieter, too.

"You don't chatter half as much as you used to, Anne," noticed Marilla one day. "What has come over you?"

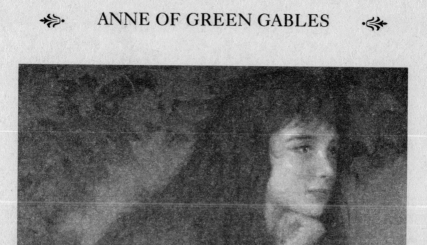

Anne laughed a little. "I don't know. I don't want to talk as much," she said. "It's nicer to keep my thoughts secret in my heart, like treasures."

"The Entrance exam is in two months," said Marilla. "Do you think you'll pass?"

Anne shivered. "I don't know. Sometimes I think I'll be all right—and then I get afraid. Geometry is so hard. I wish it was all over, Marilla. It haunts me. Sometimes I wake up at night and worry about it. I wonder what I'll do if I don't pass. It would be so awful!"

"Why, you'd go to school next year and try again," said Marilla.

"Oh, I couldn't do that. I would feel so ashamed if I failed. What if Gil—er—if all the others passed and I didn't?" Anne sighed.

The school term was over at the end of June. For Diana, this meant losing her dear deskmate.

"We had such jolly times there," said Diana, as two big tears rolled down her cheeks. "And now you'll go to Queen's next year."

"I may be back—I know I'm not going to pass the Entrance," said Anne, comforting her friend.

"You'll come out splendidly," said Diana. "You'll write to me, won't you?"

"I'll write Tuesday night and tell you how the first day of testing goes," promised Anne.

"I'll be waiting at the post office Wednesday," vowed Diana.

Anne went to the city the following Monday with Miss Stacy and the Queen's class to take the Entrance exam. And on Wednesday, Diana waited at the post office and got her letter.

Dear Diana,

Here it is Tuesday night. I'm writing this in the library. This morning, we all went to the Academy with Miss Stacy. There were lots of students there from all over the Island. We went to our rooms and Miss Stacy had to leave. We took our seats. Then a man passed out the English part of the test. My heart was beating so loudly I was sure everyone in the room could hear it. I think I did really well on the test though, once I settled down.

At noon we went to lunch, and then returned for the history test. It was a pretty hard test. I got mixed up on the dates. Still, I think I passed both tests today.

I went down to see the other girls this evening. Ruby was so upset. She thinks she made a huge mistake on the English test. Jane was her usual practical self. She talked to Ruby and Ruby settled right down. Then we went uptown and had an ice cream. We wished that you could have been here with us. We would have had so much fun!

Tomorrow is the geometry test. It scares me so! Oh, Diana, if only it was over! But life will go on, even if I fail geometry.
Yours truly,
Anne

Anne got home on Friday evening. Diana was waiting for her at Green Gables. "Oh, Anne, how did you get along?"

"Pretty well, I think, in everything but geometry. Oh, it is good to be back! Green Gables is the best place in the world."

Anne hoped she beat Gilbert Blythe on the Entrance. He wanted to beat her, too. The whole time they were in the city for the tests, they didn't talk to each other once. Every time they passed each other in the hall, both looked away.

Anne had another reason for wanting to do well. She wanted to "pass high" for Matthew and Marilla—especially Matthew, who had told her he was sure that she "would beat the whole Island."

Three weeks went by. The Entrance results would be printed in the newspaper. Anne went to the post office every day to look for them. She couldn't stand the strain much longer. She couldn't eat or sleep. She was too nervous about the test results.

One evening, the news came. Diana ran up the lane to Green Gables with a newspaper in her hand. The pass list was out! Diana burst into Anne's room without even knocking.

"Anne, you've *all* passed," she cried. "You and Gilbert tied for first place! Oh, I'm so proud!"

Anne grabbed the paper. Yes, she had passed! There was her name at the very top of the list! That was a moment worth living for. And there was Gilbert Blythe's name right next to hers.

"You did just splendidly, Anne," gushed Diana. "Won't Miss Stacy be delighted? How does it feel?"

"I'm just dazzled inside," said Anne. "I never dreamed of this. Yes, I did too, just once! Excuse me a minute, Diana. I must run to tell Matthew. Then we'll go up the road and tell the good news to the others."

They hurried to the hayfield to find Matthew. Mrs. Lynde was talking to Marilla at the fence.

"Oh, Matthew," said Anne, "I've passed and I'm first—or one of the first!"

"Well now, I always said it," said Matthew. He looked at the list with a big smile. "I knew you could beat them all easy."

"You've done pretty well, I must say, Anne," said Marilla, trying to hide her pride in Anne from Rachel Lynde.

Mrs. Lynde agreed. "You're a credit to your friends, Anne, and we're all proud of you."

151

That night, Anne sat for a while by her open window. She said a prayer of thanks, straight from the heart. Her future was rosy! When she slept, her dreams were bright and beautiful.

CHAPTER THIRTEEN

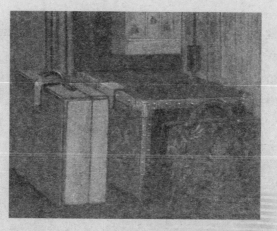

A Queen's Girl

The next three weeks were busy ones at Green Gables. Anne was getting ready to go to Queen's. They had many things to talk over and arrange. Marilla thought back to the first night Anne came to Green Gables. She had been such a frightened little girl. Something in the memory brought tears to Marilla's eyes.

"Why are you crying, Marilla?" asked Anne.

"I was just thinking of the little girl you used to be, Anne. I was wishing you could have stayed a little girl, even with all your odd ways. You've grown up and now you're going away. I just got lonesome thinking about it."

"Marilla," Anne said gently, "the real me is just the same. I'll always be your little Anne at heart. I'll always love you and Matthew and dear Green Gables."

Matthew wiped away a tear and went outside. "Well now, I guess she ain't been much spoiled," he thought. "She's been a blessing to us. There never was a luckier mistake than what Mrs. Spencer made—if it was luck. God saw we needed her, I reckon."

The day finally came for Anne to leave for Queen's. It was so hard to say good-bye to Diana and Marilla! Matthew drove her to Charlottetown that fine September morning.

Anne's first day was exciting. She met lots of new students. Anne and Gilbert both signed up for the advanced classes. This meant that they would be able to teach in just one year. It also meant much harder work.

Anne felt lonesome when she first went into class. The only other person she knew was Gilbert, and he didn't count. Still, it was nice to know that someone from home was there. She was glad that she could still compete with him for the best grades.

Anne was lonesomer still when she went to her room that evening. The other girls had relatives in town to live with, but Anne was staying at a boarding house. Everything in the city was so different! She started to cry.

Suddenly, Josie, Jane, and Ruby knocked on her door. They were full of news of their first day. Ruby asked Anne if she was going to try to win the Gold Medal for best student. Anne blushed and said yes. Josie told them that Queen's was also going to give the Avery scholarship.

The Avery! The best English literature student would receive two hundred and fifty dollars a year to pay for four years at Redmond College. Anne's heart beat faster.

"I'll win that scholarship if hard work can do it," Anne decided. "Wouldn't Matthew and Marilla be proud? It's delightful to have grand plans. It makes life so interesting."

After Christmas, the deep snows set in. All the students settled into their class work. Gilbert, Anne, and another boy were at the top of the class. One of them would surely win the Gold Medal. There were six students who might win the Avery scholarship.

Anne worked hard. She still liked to compete with Gilbert, but she didn't feel as angry about it anymore. She just liked to win for winning's sake. She was happy for Gilbert when he did well.

Almost before they knew it, spring had come. Out in Avonlea, Mayflowers were blooming, and a mist of green was on the woods and in the valleys. But in Charlottetown, tired Queen's students worried about their end of year tests.

Three days after they took the tests, the scores were posted. Anne and Jane walked to Queen's Academy together. Anne was pale and quiet. In a few minutes, she would know if she had won the medal or the Avery scholarship.

When they went into Queen's, they saw boys carrying Gilbert Blythe on their shoulders. They were all yelling, "Hurrah for Gilbert! He won the Gold Medal!"

For a moment, Anne was disappointed. She had failed—and Gilbert had won. Matthew would be sorry. He was so sure she would win.

And then somebody called out, "Three cheers for Miss Shirley, winner of the Avery!"

"Oh, Anne," gasped Jane. "Oh, Anne, I'm so proud! Isn't it splendid?"

160

The students gathered around Anne. They shook her hands and patted her shoulders. Everyone was laughing. Anne was pushed and pulled and hugged. She whispered to Jane, "Oh, won't Matthew and Marilla be pleased!"

At graduation, Matthew and Marilla only had eyes and ears for Anne.

"Reckon you're glad we kept her, Marilla?" whispered Matthew.

"It's not the first time I've been glad," retorted Marilla. "You do like to rub things in, Matthew Cuthbert."

Anne went home to Avonlea that night. Diana was at Green Gables to meet her.

"Oh, Diana, it's so good to be back again," Anne said. "And it's good to see you again! Tomorrow, I'm going to just play in the orchard and not think at all."

The next morning at breakfast, Anne thought Matthew looked sort of gray. "Marilla," she asked later, "is Matthew feeling well?"

"No, he isn't," said Marilla, worried. "He's had some real bad spells with his heart this spring. He just keeps working so hard. Maybe he'll rest now that you're home. You always cheer him up."

Anne smiled at Marilla. "You don't look so very well yourself, Marilla. I'm worried about you. You've been working too hard. You must take a rest now that I'm home. I'm going to take this one day off to play. Then it will be your turn to be lazy while I do the work."

Marilla smiled at her girl. "It's not the work. It's my headaches. The pain is right behind my eyes. The doctor gave me glasses, but they don't do any good. I can hardly read or sew. Something else is worrying Matthew," Marilla continued. "The Abbey Bank is shaky. All our money is in that bank. I wanted Matthew to draw our money out, but he didn't. Mr. Russell at the bank told him yesterday that everything would be all right."

Anne had her good day off. She never forgot that day. She spent some of it in the orchard. She walked along the Lake of Shining Waters. She had a long talk with Mrs. Allan. At sunset, she went with Matthew to bring the cows in. Matthew walked very slowly.

"You've been working too hard, Matthew," she said. "Why won't you take it easy?"

"Well now, I can't seem to," said Matthew. "It's only that I'm getting old, Anne. I've always worked

pretty hard and I don't know how to stop."

"If I had been a boy," said Anne, "I'd be able to help you so much now."

"Well now, I'd rather have you than a dozen boys, Anne," said Matthew. "It wasn't a boy that took the Avery, was it? It was a girl—my girl—my girl that I'm proud of." He smiled his shy smile at her as he went into the yard.

Anne always remembered the peaceful beauty of that night. It was the last night before sorrow touched her life.

CHAPTER FOURTEEN

A Bend in the Road

"Matthew, what is the matter? Matthew, are you sick?" Marilla asked urgently.

Matthew was standing at the door with a newspaper in his hand. His face was an odd gray color. Anne and Marilla both ran to him. Before they could get there, Matthew fell to the floor.

Anne ran to send for the doctor. Marilla knelt beside Matthew. She patted his cheeks and stroked his face. She could not wake him up.

When the doctor came, he said that Matthew had died instantly. He had not been in any pain. The doctor said that a sudden shock must have caused it.

When they looked at the newspaper, they learned what the shock was. The Abbey Bank had failed. All of the Cuthberts' money was gone.

News of Matthew's death spread quickly through town. All day, friends and neighbors called at Green Gables.

Poor Anne did not cry at all. She spent the whole day feeling a burning ache inside. It almost choked her. When she went to bed that night, she hoped she could cry. She had loved Matthew so much. He had been so kind to her. Why couldn't she cry for him? But no tears came.

In the middle of the night, Anne woke up. She remembered all that had happened. She could hear Matthew's voice saying, "My girl, my girl that I'm proud of." Then the tears came and Anne wept her heart out.

Two days later they buried Matthew Cuthbert. Things in Avonlea settled down. Even at Green Gables things got back to normal. But it would never really be normal again without Matthew. Grief was new to Anne. She felt almost ashamed when she enjoyed the sunrises and sunsets. She felt guilty when she laughed with Diana.

Anne went to visit Mrs. Allan. She told her how she was feeling.

"Matthew always liked it when you were happy," said Mrs. Allan gently. "He is just away now and he still likes it. I understand your feelings. I think we all feel that way. Sometimes we almost feel guilty when we enjoy life after someone dies."

"I planted a rosebush on Matthew's grave this afternoon," said Anne. "Matthew always liked roses the best. I hope he has roses in heaven."

The next day, the special eye doctor came to town. He examined Marilla's eyes. Marilla looked very sad when she came home from seeing him.

"Are you very tired, Marilla?" Anne asked. "What did the doctor say?"

"He says I have to give up any kind of work that strains my eyes. If I do, my eyes may not get any worse. My headaches may be cured. But if I don't, he says I'll be blind in six months. Blind! What am I to live for if I can't read or sew or do anything?"

How Anne's life had changed! Matthew gone and Marilla going blind! That night, Anne made up her mind. She knew what she must do.

A few days later, Marilla told Anne that she was going to sell Green Gables. Anne would be off to college in the fall. Marilla, with her eyes going blind, could not manage the farm. They had lost their savings when the Abbey Bank failed. Selling Green Gables was the only thing she could do. Marilla wept as she told this to Anne.

"You don't have to sell Green Gables," said Anne. "You won't have to stay here alone, Marilla. I'll be with you. I'm not going to Redmond College.

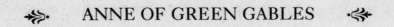

How could I leave you alone after all you've done for me? Let me tell you my plans. Mr. Barry wants to rent the farm for next year. And I'm going to teach. The Avonlea school has been promised to Gilbert, but I can get another nearby school. I have it all planned out, Marilla."

"Oh, Anne, I can't let you give up all your dreams for me," Marilla answered.

"Nonsense!" Anne laughed. "Nothing could be worse than giving up Green Gables. My mind is made up. I'm going to be a good teacher and I'm going to save your eyesight. When I left Queen's, my future looked like a straight road. Now there is a bend in it. I don't know what lies around the bend, but I'm sure that the best does."

Mrs. Lynde heard about Anne's change of plans. She came to talk to her.

"Well, Anne," Mrs. Lynde said, "I hear you're not going to college."

"Yes," Anne replied. "I'm going to teach over at the school in Carmody."

"No, you're not. You're going to teach right here in Avonlea. The trustees are giving you the school."

"Mrs. Lynde," said Anne, "you must be wrong. I heard that they promised it to Gilbert Blythe!"

"Gilbert withdrew his application and told them to accept yours. He's going to teach at White Sands. He knows how much you want to stay with Marilla. He's already signed the papers, so it's all set."

Anne went to the graveyard the next evening. She put fresh flowers on Matthew's grave and watered the rosebush. She listened to the leaves rustle, and then turned slowly, dreamily, down the lane, noticing all the quiet beauty around her. "Dear old world," she murmured, "you are very lovely, and I am glad to be alive in you."

As she walked back to Green Gables, she met Gilbert on the road. He politely tipped his cap and walked on by. Anne reached out to stop him.

"Gilbert," she said, "thank you for giving up the school for me. It was very good of you."

"I was pleased to do it, Anne. Are we going to be friends after all? Have you forgiven me for teasing you about your hair?"

Anne laughed. "I forgave you that day when you rescued me at the bridge, but I didn't realize it. What a stubborn little goose I was!"

"We are going to be the best of friends," said Gilbert. "We were born to be good friends, Anne. Come, I'll walk you home."

172

Marilla looked curiously at Anne when she entered the kitchen.

"Who came up the lane with you, Anne?"

"Gilbert Blythe," said Anne, blushing.

"I didn't think you and Gilbert were such good friends that you'd stand for half an hour at the gate talking to him," said Marilla with a smile.

"We haven't been—we've been good enemies. But we've decided to be good friends from now on. Were we really there half an hour? It seemed just a few minutes. We have so much to catch up on… five years' worth."

That night, Anne looked out of the east gable window. The wind purred in the cherry tree's branches and the stars twinkled over the fir trees in the valley. She knew that she had made the right choice to stay here. She knew that a narrow but happy path lay before her, with hard work, friendship, and dreams. And there was always the bend in the road.

" 'God's in His heaven, all's right with the world,' " Anne whispered softly.

175

L.M. MONTGOMERY

Lucy Maud Montgomery was born on Canada's Prince Edward Island in 1874. She was raised by her grandmother in a farmhouse in the town of Cavendish. Montgomery began writing poems and stories at a young age. At twelve she won a short story contest sponsored by a Montreal newspaper. In her teens, she attended college for one year and then returned to Prince Edward Island to teach school.

She published *Anne of Green Gables* in 1908. It was her first novel and quickly gained legions of fans. Anne Shirley was such a popular heroine that Montgomery continued her adventures in seven more novels (*Anne of Avonlea, Anne of the Island, Anne of Windy Poplars, Anne's House of Dreams, Anne of Ingleside, Rainbow Valley,* and *Rilla of Ingleside*). Altogether, Montgomery published twenty novels and about 500 short stories and poems. Nineteen of the novels were set on her beloved Prince Edward Island.

At the age of 37, three years after she published *Anne of Green Gables*, Montgomery married the Reverend Ewan MacDonald. She lived in Ontario, Canada, after her marriage and died in Toronto in 1942.